LIN OLIVER

THE FANTASTIC FRAME

For my great friend Etta Kralovec, who, like Georgia,
fights for women and loves the desert—LO

For Mary-Lou, Werner, Trudy, and Albert,
with my love and gratitude—SK

PENGUIN WORKSHOP
An Imprint of Penguin Random House LLC, New York

Text copyright © 2017 by Lin Oliver. Illustrations copyright © 2017 by
Samantha Kallis. All rights reserved. Previously published in hardcover in 2017
by Grosset & Dunlap. This paperback edition published in 2019 by Penguin Workshop, an
imprint of Penguin Random House LLC, New York. PENGUIN and PENGUIN WORKSHOP
are trademarks of Penguin Books Ltd, and the W colophon is a registered trademark of
Penguin Random House LLC. Manufactured in China.

Visit us online at www.penguinrandomhouse.com.

Library of Congress Control Number: 2017006026

ISBN 9780448480923 | 10 9 8 7 6 5 4 3 2 1

THE FANTASTIC FRAME

Look Out! Ghost Mountain Below

BY **LIN OLIVER**

ILLUSTRATED BY
SAMANTHA KALLIS

Penguin Workshop

PROLOGUE

Hi, it's Tiger Brooks. Got a second? Good, because I have a few thoughts about neighbors that I'd like to share with you.

Here's something I've noticed in my ten years on this planet: Every neighborhood has at least one really weird person in it.

I bet you've got one in your neighborhood. It might be someone with a ton of gnome statues on their lawn. Or someone who sings to the vegetables in their garden. Or maybe it's someone who puts little red rain boots on their dog.

On my old block, there was a woman who had a pet tortoise named Speedo. She took Speedo out for a walk every day . . . on a leash! It took them most of the day to make it to the corner and back.

My dad says when he was young, he had a neighbor named Louie who collected balls. Golf balls, soccer balls, tennis balls, footballs, volleyballs, Ping-Pong balls, Wiffle balls, you name it. If my dad and his friends were playing and a ball went into Louie's yard, he kept it. They called him Old Louie the Ball Eater.

I promise you, no one in the world has a neighbor weirder than mine. Her name is Viola Dots. She lives in a run-down house right next to our duplex. She's almost eighty years old and hasn't left her house in fifty years! All she does is paint copies of great works of art. Oh, and did I mention that she has a talking orange pig named Chives who's her butler?

But that's not even the weirdest part.

The strangest thing about Viola Dots is that she has a magical picture frame in her living room. At four o'clock, which we call the hour of power, this frame is able to suck you into the picture if you're standing nearby. You go flying across time and space into whatever artwork is in the frame. If you're not back at the same place by five o'clock, you're stuck in the painting forever. That's what happened to Viola's son, David, fifty years ago. And that's why she paints all day, every day . . . She's hoping that he'll show up in her paintings.

Viola's fantastic frame is a secret. Only Chives, my friend Luna Lopez, and I know about it. And, of course, you. But you have to keep it a secret, because if you don't, people will come to her house and try to take the magical frame. She doesn't want that. At least, not until she finds David.

So you have to promise to keep the fantastic frame a secret. Can you do that?

Good. If you can, then read on. If you can't, pretend you never read this.

CHAPTER 1

The ghost crept closer and closer, its eyes glowing red. It had no bones, only a hollow body that seemed to be made of swirling fog. I could see through its long arms as they reached out to grab me. A chill ran down my spine.

"I am coming to get you," the ghost cried.

A slimy fluid poured out of the hole where its mouth should have been. My heart was beating wildly. Suddenly, something moved on the couch next to me, and I jumped about ten feet in the air.

It was my friend, Luna Lopez.

"Okay, Tiger, I'll be changing the channel now," she said, standing up from the couch and clicking the remote control.

"But, Luna, we're not even at the good part where the ghost freaks out."

"I can't watch this, Tiger," she said. "It's way too creepy. I like my ghosts in a good mood. The same way I like my mummies, my vampires, and my werewolves."

"But it's fun to be scared. It's just a movie."

It was a Thursday night and my parents were at an open house at Rainbow Years, my little sister Maggie's preschool. The four-year-old class was putting on a skit, and Maggie was playing a mushroom in the forest. I thought it was a great part for her, because she reminds me of a fungus. Our babysitter was busy, so my mom asked Luna's grandmother if she could watch me until they got home. Señora Lopez had fallen asleep in her rocking chair.

"Come on, Luna, just give it five more minutes," I urged.

"Okay," she said. "But I'm warning you. The minute that spooky phantom moans again, I'm out of here."

We settled on the couch to watch the movie. The ghost had calmed down and was just floating outside the haunted house, looking in the windows. The only sounds in the room were Luna's grandmother snoring and the scary music coming from the TV. Suddenly, we heard a noise by the living room window. *Clink-clink-clink* followed by the rattle of the windowpane.

"What's that?" Luna whispered. There was a little panic in her voice.

It sounded like someone was throwing rocks at the window. We waited, hoping the rock thrower had left. But then we heard it again. *Clink-clink-clink*.

"I'm going to check it out," I said.

"I'm coming with you." Luna picked up a throw pillow from the couch. "If it's a ghost, I'll swat him with this."

"If it's really a ghost, that pillow's going to

go right through him," I pointed out.

We crept over to the window and looked out, just as three more pebbles hit the glass in front of us. It was dark outside, and I couldn't make out who was standing below. I opened the window a crack.

"Who's down there?" I called out.

"If you're a ghost, go away," Luna added.

"It is I," said a familiar voice. "Chives. I must speak with you two right away about an urgent matter."

"Chives," I said in my loudest whisper. "What are you doing out?"

"At the risk of repeating myself, young sir, I must see you immediately on a matter of great importance."

I glanced over at Señora Lopez, who was still asleep in the chair. Luna and I tiptoed past her and hurried down the stairs. We found Chives standing in the driveway, pacing back and forth. He is always calm. It was not like him to be this upset.

"It's Madame Dots," he said, taking out a handkerchief and blowing his snout. "I'm terribly worried about her."

"What's wrong with her?" Luna asked.

"I made her a cup of rose hips tea this afternoon," Chives said. "She is always in the living room, painting, but when I brought it to her today, she was gone."

"Maybe she finally decided to go outside and get some sun," I said. "No offense, Chives, but a little sunshine wouldn't hurt her."

"Tiger, that's so rude," Luna whispered, giving me a poke in the ribs.

"I searched every room and finally discovered her in young Master David's bedroom," Chives went on. "She's kept that room locked since he disappeared into the fantastic frame."

"What was she doing in there?" Luna asked.

"Touching everything on his shelves," Chives answered. "His collections of records, arrowheads, geodes, and model cars."

"Maybe she was just cleaning," I suggested. "My mom is always threatening to go into my room and clean all the junk off my shelves. Last week she threw out my rubber-band collection."

"No, Madame Dots was definitely looking for something," Chives said. "I stayed with her for hours, until she found what she was looking for."

"What was it?" Luna and I both asked at once.

"A birthday card," Chives said with a

sniffle, "that her son, David, was making for her on the day he disappeared. She said she had to see it again."

"You mean, he disappeared on her birthday?" Luna asked. "How horrible."

"Yes." Chives nodded his head. "Tomorrow it will be fifty years. And tomorrow she will turn eighty years old."

"What a sad birthday that will be for her," Luna said.

"Yes indeed," Chives agreed. "Unless, of course, you two can bring David home to her. Then it will be a day of great celebration."

"Wow, no pressure there," I said.

Luna poked me in the ribs again. I guess I was having a rude kind of day.

"Does Mrs. Dots have a finished painting

ready for us to enter tomorrow?" Luna asked. "Maybe we can find David."

"I believe so," Chives said. "It's a copy of a beautiful piece done in 1936 by the American artist Georgia O'Keeffe. It's called *Red Hills with the Pedernal*, and it's a painting of a famous mountain in New Mexico."

"That sounds exciting," I said. "Bring on the hour of power!"

"I've never climbed a mountain," Luna said. "But I'm willing to try if we think David might be there."

"This is a very special mountain," Chives explained. "It is sacred to many Native American tribes, like the Navajo. Some tribes even believe it is home to important spirits."

"Spirits?" Luna said with a shudder. "You

don't mean like ghosts, do you?"

Before Chives could answer, we saw headlights coming down our street and heard three quick taps of a horn. That's my dad's special honk.

"My parents are back," I said to Chives. "Hurry or they'll see you."

"Until tomorrow then," Chives said. "We will meet at the fantastic frame at four o'clock, the hour of power, with brave thoughts and high expectations."

He tipped his top hat, turned, and ran down the driveway, slipping into the side door of Viola's house just as our car pulled up. Maggie, the little blabbermouth, stuck her head out of the car window.

"I see you!" she hollered. "I see you, Mr. Orange Pig."

Of course, my parents didn't see him. You only see an orange pig if you're looking for one. My mom lifted Maggie out of her car seat and rubbed her mushroomy head.

"Maggie has seen lots of imaginary creatures tonight," she laughed. "Unicorns and elves and dragons and trolls. The forest was full of them. Wasn't it, honey?"

"That pig wasn't in my imagination," Maggie insisted.

"Four-year-olds," I said. "Who knows what's in their goofy little heads?"

Luna and I laughed, a bit too hard.

"Let's go wash the moss out of your hair," my mom said to Maggie. "Maybe we'll see Mr. Pig in the bathtub."

I felt a little bad that my mom didn't believe Maggie. But then, it's hard to believe a talking mushroom.

"I thought you kids were going to watch a movie," my dad said.

"We started to, but it was a ghost movie and we decided to turn it off."

"Oh, got a tad scared, did you?" my dad asked. "Well, things that go bump in the night can be pretty scary."

"Those things aren't real, are they, Mr. Brooks?" Luna asked. "Like phantoms and ghosts . . . they don't really exist. I mean, they wouldn't actually live on, oh let's say, a mountain in New Mexico, would they?"

"I've never been to New Mexico," my dad said. "The natural world is full of stories about all kinds of amazing things. You never know what you're going to find until you're there. But hey, nothing for us to worry about. We're not in New Mexico."

It was dark and I couldn't see Luna's face.

But I was pretty sure I heard her gulp.

CHAPTER 2

When I got dressed for school the next
morning, I put on my down vest that I
wear when we go camping. I had read
about mountain climbing on the Internet.
It said that the weather gets colder the
higher you go. I wanted to be prepared for
anything.

I came into the kitchen for breakfast
and found my mom already mixing up a
big batch of chocolate cake batter. Her
business is called Cakes by Cookie because

her name is Cookie and she bakes cakes for people's parties. Maggie was sitting at the kitchen table, whining about wanting to lick the spatula. She thinks she's my mom's assistant, and spatula-licking is her job.

"Good morning, sweetie," my mom said to me. "You're going to be awfully hot in that vest. It's supposed to be ninety degrees today."

"You never know when it can suddenly turn cold." That was a weak answer, but it was early and I'm not the best thinker in the mornings. "You look busy," I said.

"It's a four-cake day." She handed Maggie the spatula. "One anniversary, one homecoming, and two birthdays."

That gave me an idea.

"Hey, Mom, do you have enough batter

for a fifth cake?" I asked. "Just a little

birthday cake."

"I think I can squeeze out a small one,"

she said. "Is one of your friends having a

"I guess you could say that."

"Fine. Tell me your friend's name, and I'll write a 'Happy Birthday' message on the cake."

"It's Viola," I said.

My mom turned off her electric mixer and came to sit next to me.

"And this Viola, is she in your class at school?"

"Not really. She's a little older than me."

"Is she on your soccer team?"

"No, she's not a fast runner."

"Tiger," my mom said, giving me the look she saves for serious conversations. "The only Viola I know is the woman next door. The one who never leaves her house."

"Eewww," Maggie said. "Everyone says she's a mean old witch."

"Who says that?" I snapped.

"That boy down the street, Cooper Starr, told me that if I ever got near her, she would put a spell on me and turn me into a warty frog," Maggie said.

"You shouldn't listen to Cooper Starr," I told her. "He doesn't have a good thing to say about anyone. By the way, you have a big blob of chocolate on your nose."

Maggie stuck her tongue out and tried to lick the chocolate off her nose. She has a long tongue and almost made it.

"Tiger, how do you know Viola?"

My mom sounded concerned. "And how do you know it's her birthday?"

"The orange pig probably told him." Maggie giggled.

She had no idea how right she was.

"Luna and I say hi to Viola on the way home from school," I said. That was sort of true. We do always say hi to her. I just left out the little detail about us time-traveling into her paintings.

"I see," my mom said. "Well, I'm sure she's very lonely. I'll bake a cake for her and maybe we can take it over this afternoon. I'd like to meet her."

"Speaking of this afternoon, Mom, I'm going to be home late from school. Luna and I have a special project to finish."

That was true, too. Sort of.

"Oh, what's it about?" my mom asked.

"New Mexico."

I grabbed my lunch, gave my mom a kiss, and headed out the door. Luna was waiting for me on the driveway. She had dressed for New Mexico, too . . . but in a very Luna way. She was wearing a headband decorated with shells and carrying a drum on her back. It was a small drum with pieces of colored leather woven along the sides and the strap.

"I made the headband last night from my seashell collection," Luna said. "Pretty cool, huh?"

"What about the drum?" I asked. "Do you have a drum collection, too?"

"Of course," Luna said. "Doesn't everyone?"

My dad has a harmonica, but that's about it for our family's musical-instrument collection.

"My grandpa Arturo made this drum as a present for my grandma," Luna went on. "He said that no matter where he was, she could feel his heartbeat in the drum. She lets me borrow it."

Normally I don't like a lot of lovey-dovey kind of talk, but even I had to admit that was a pretty nice thing to say.

"You didn't tell your grandma that we were planning to travel to New Mexico, did you?" I asked.

We had sworn to Viola that we would always keep the secret of her magic frame. The last thing she wanted was for anyone to come and take it away. That would end all her hopes of ever finding David.

"Don't worry, Tiger," Luna said. "I didn't tell her anything. But it makes me feel safe to know that Grandpa Arturo's drum is with me."

As we walked down the driveway and passed Viola's house, we looked up and saw Chives in the third-floor window.

You couldn't see all of him, just his snout and bow tie, and one eye peeking out. We knew he was watching us, probably counting the hours until four o'clock when we would enter the fantastic frame.

With any luck, we would find David on the mountain and convince him to come home to his mother.

That would give Viola Dots the happiest birthday of her life.

CHAPTER 3

At lunch that day, Luna and I met in the school library to read up on Georgia O'Keeffe and her painting. By the time I got there, Luna had already asked our librarian, Mrs. Kim, to help her find a book on American artists. Luna was sitting at a table, flipping through the pages.

"Georgia O'Keeffe sure loved to paint flowers," she said.

She slid the book over so I could see it. I went past the colorful flowers until I came to the paintings of New Mexico. I saw white cliffs and red hills, but I couldn't find the painting of the mountain Chives had described.

"What was it called again?" I asked Luna.

"*Red Hills with the Pedernal*, I think."

"Is *pedernal* a Spanish word?"

"Sounds like it," Luna said, "but I don't know what it means."

We asked Mrs. Kim for help finding the right page, and she showed us how to look it up in the index. There it was. Cerro Pedernal, page 97.

"*Cerro* means *hill* in Spanish," Luna said.

"That's more than a hill." We studied the picture of Cerro Pedernal. It was a huge mountain, towering over the red and green

and brown valley below. What was so unusual about it, though, was its peak. It wasn't pointed at the top, like most mountains. It was completely flat, like the blade of a knife.

"Cerro Pedernal looks like its top fell off," I said to Luna.

"It says in the caption that it's called a butte," Luna read. "That's a tall steep mountain with a small flat top. Pedernal's top is made of flint, which is a kind of stone that Native peoples used to make arrowheads and tools."

"Arrowheads!" I said. "Chives told us that David collected arrowheads."

"Then if he's there, we'll know where to find him," Luna said. "At the top, looking for more arrowheads for his collection."

"Oh look," I said, glancing down the page. "It says here that Georgia O'Keeffe lived close to the real Pedernal, on a ranch they called Ghost Ranch."

As soon as those words left my mouth, I wanted to take them back. Why did I have to mention ghosts, when I knew the whole topic scared Luna?

"Did you say 'Ghost Ranch'?" Luna asked, just like I knew she would. "I don't like the sound of that."

"We're not actually going to Ghost Ranch," I said, trying to sound cheerful.

just gives me the creeps."

We quietly walked home, preparing ourselves for the afternoon's adventure. As we turned up our street, I heard a cackling noise behind us, like someone was doing a bad imitation of a chicken laying an egg. Then came that all-too-familiar voice. It was Cooper Starr.

"Hey, losers," he said, pulling his bike up on the sidewalk and riding alongside us. "You two are looking even worse than usual today. I like your drum, loony Luna. What'd you do, join a weirdo band?"

"Cooper, just go away," I said.

"Are you guys going to visit your favorite witch again?" he jeered.

"Viola Dots is a whole lot more interesting than you are," I said.

"What if I won't let you go?" Cooper said. He pulled his bike in front of us, blocking our path so we couldn't get past. "What are you going to do about that, huh?"

Luna stood up very straight and put her hands on her hips. She moved in about one inch from Cooper's face.

"Cooper Starr, you're just being mean," she said. "And in case no one ever told you, it's not nice to be mean."

Cooper looked surprised.

"Who do you think you are?" He snarled.

"I'm Luna Lopez," she said. "And listen up, Cooper, because I'm counting from ten, and you'd better be gone by the time I reach one."

"Or what?" Cooper said.

"Let's just say it involves my dad, who is really big and strong," Luna said. "Ten . . . nine . . . eight . . ."

Cooper is a bully, but he's not brave. By the time Luna reached three, he was pedaling away from us.

"Luna," I said when he was out of sight.

"Your dad isn't even here. He's in Texas with his army unit."

"I know that, and you know that," she said. "But Cooper Starr doesn't know that."

"You've got guts," I said to her.

"Yup," she said with a smile. "I am brave."

By the time we reached Viola's house, it was close to four o'clock. We knocked on her door. Usually, we hear Chives's hoof steps scurrying to open the door for us. But today, it was silent inside.

I picked up the paintbrush-shaped knocker and pounded the door again. There was still no answer.

"Chives!" Luna called out. "Open up! It's us."

We waited another minute and knocked again.

"Chives!" I called. "Hurry! We're going to run out of time."

It seemed like forever until the door slowly swung open, just enough to let us look inside.

We couldn't believe what we saw.

CHAPTER 4

It was Chives at the door, but not the Chives we knew.

The Chives we knew was always perfectly dressed in his top hat and polka-dot bow tie. He always wore a jacket and a white shirt and formal black pants. He never appeared as anything but a perfect gentleman, even though he was a pig.

But this Chives looked like a combination of Johnny Appleseed and Bozo the Clown. He was wearing a tank top and hiking shorts with a yellow plastic bucket on his head. And to top off the whole look, he was carrying a mop.

I would have said something, but my mouth was hanging too far open to talk.

"Chives," Luna sputtered. "What happened to you? Did you fall into a junk pile?"

"Hurry inside," he said. "I will explain everything."

We entered the house. From the living room, we could hear Mrs. Dots's voice.

"Is that the children, Chives?" she shouted. "Bring them to me *immediately.*"

"Yes, Madame," Chives called out. "We will be right in."

He stood close to us and whispered. "I imagine you're wondering why I am dressed this way," he began. "This is my mountain-climbing outfit. Not having proper clothes at my disposal, I have pieced this together from common objects I found around the house."

"A bucket and a mop?" I said. "Those will help you wash the floors, but not climb a mountain."

"Perhaps they look like a bucket and a mop to you," Chives said, "but to me, they are my helmet and my walking stick."

"I don't understand," Luna said. "Where are you going mountain climbing?"

"I am going with you into the fantastic frame," he answered. "You two have searched for David several times now, yet he has never agreed to return with you. I believe that if we are lucky enough to find him on Pedernal, I can bring him home."

"I'm not so sure he wants to come back," I said. I had been thinking that for a while, but I had never had the nerve to say it.

"It is time for David to come home," Chives said. "For fifty years, I have stood by and watched my mistress suffer. If I can explain to David how much his mother misses him, I believe he will return. Now we must hurry, children."

We ran into the living room and found Viola Dots staring at the huge golden frame. Inside the frame was her painting of Cerro Pedernal. It was an awesome sight. The mountain rose like a volcano above a low brown valley covered with green bushes and red soil.

"Finally, you're here," Viola said without turning around. "Just in time."

The clock on the bottom of the frame said it was two minutes to four. The hour of power was about to begin. Mrs. Dots was calling out directions in her usual bossy tone.

"Now, if you find David, I want you to tell him . . ."

As she turned to face us, she caught

sight of Chives. She let out a loud gasp.

"Good heavens, Chives. What on earth has happened to you?"

"I have decided to accompany the children into the frame to search for Master David," he said.

"How can you help, Chives?" she snapped. "You're just a pig."

"But he's a very loving pig," Luna said. "He wants to bring David home for your birthday. You should say thank you. My grandmother says that 'thank you' is the most important thing you can say to anyone."

"I thank Chives every day . . . for bringing me tea, for fixing me dinner, for taking care of the house. Don't I, Chives?"

"Well, perhaps not every day, Madame. But I do believe you thanked me once."

"Then it's settled," Viola said. "You're not going. I need you here."

"My decision is firm, Madame," Chives said. "I am going forth. It is my duty and my honor."

He walked over to the golden frame and stood bravely in front of it. No sooner had he taken his position in front of the painting than the clock on the frame started to chime.

"Are you ready?" I asked Luna, reaching out for her hand.

"I am brave," she said, grasping my hand tightly in hers.

"Let the adventure begin!" Chives shouted, raising his mop high in the air.

I looked at the painting and saw a small hole beginning to open up. I had hoped it would be at the top of the mountain, but it wasn't. It was in the valley below, in a patch of what appeared to be rusty red hills.

I heard the sound of the canvas ripping apart. I felt myself being pulled toward the painting. I thought I felt sand and dust on my face. I didn't resist.

I was ready to go.

CHAPTER 5

The whole living room trembled beneath
my feet. I could hear Viola's voice, but it was
growing distant.

"Bring my son back to me," she called.
"Please, bring him back. Thank you,
children. Thank you, Chives."

Her voice faded away, and all I could
hear was the whistling of wind. It grew
louder and louder as the hole grew bigger
and bigger. Somewhere in the air around me,
a man was singing in a different language.

Luna reached out for Chives and grabbed him by the hoof.

"I've got you," I heard her say. "I won't let go."

Everything around me began to grow blurry. The white walls and sparkling chandeliers of Viola's living room disappeared. Colors swirled before my eyes . . . rusty reds, dark greens, purples and blues. Around and around they spun until I could see no forms at all, just color.

I was swept off my feet and into the hole in the painting. Luna was by my side, clutching my hand as we hurtled through time and space. Chives was next to her. I could see him gripping his mop and trying to hold the yellow plastic bucket on his head.

I don't know how long we tumbled or
how far. All I know is that when I landed,

I was on the side of a dusty gravel road, covered in red dirt. I sat up, rubbed my eyes, and looked around. Luna was lying in the dust beside me, the drum still strapped to her back. Chives was nowhere to be seen.

The sun beat down on us. A hot wind rustled in the nearby pine trees. Looming in the distance was Cerro Pedernal, jutting straight up to the sky and appearing even larger than it did in the painting. It was a scary and beautiful mountain, glowing with an almost ghostly light.

Slowly, I became aware of the sound of a car sputtering down the road. It was an old gray pickup truck, kicking up a cloud of dust as it made its way along the bumpy road. The driver was singing the same song I had heard in the tunnel.

I could only see the outline of the man
in the driver's seat. He wore a big straw hat
that cast a shadow over his face. I couldn't
tell if he was smiling or frowning.

The truck pulled up alongside us and stopped.

The man in the straw hat got out. He had long black hair that flowed out from beneath his hat. He was tall and wore silver bracelets with turquoise stones in them.

"You lost, boy?" he asked.

"I don't think so," I answered. "This is New Mexico, isn't it?"

"Yup."

"That's a nice old truck you got there," I said.

He scowled at me, obviously angry at something I had said.

"My truck isn't old," he snapped. "I bought it this year."

"No way," I said. "Look at those chrome headlights and that classic grille. Your truck looks like it's straight out of an old movie."

I felt Luna's elbow in my ribs.

"Tiger," she whispered. "Remember, we're in the painting. It's 1936."

Of course, I had totally forgotten.

"I'm Tiger Brooks," I said, sticking out my hand. "And this is my friend Luna."

"I'm Rio," the man answered, almost crushing my hand in his strong grip. "That means river in Spanish."

"*Yo sé*," Luna said. "*Yo hablo Español.* My family is from Mexico. Are you?"

"No, I am Navajo," he said. "My tribe has lived in New Mexico for many hundreds of years. I was born and raised right here in the badlands, a stone's throw from Ghost Ranch."

Luna's face immediately clouded over with worry.

"Excuse me, sir," she said, "but did you say b-b-badlands? Can you tell us what's so bad about them? I mean, there aren't any bad spirits here, are there?"

"Depends on what you mean by spirits," Rio answered.

Oh boy, that was not the answer Luna was hoping for.

"You mentioned Ghost Ranch," Luna said. "So I was just wondering if maybe there are ghosts here, or any other spirits you think I should know about."

"The Navajo people used to believe that Cerro Pedernal is home to the goddess we call Changing Woman, who grows old and young again with the seasons," Rio said. "The story goes that she created our people from the skin of her body."

"Oh, so she's a good spirit, then," Luna said, sounding relieved. "She wouldn't hurt anyone."

"She is always kind," Rio answered. "Not like the evil skinwalkers that many say live on Pedernal."

Did he say evil skinwalkers? No! Tell me he didn't say evil skinwalkers!!!!

"Excuse me, Rio," I said. "I don't think I heard you correctly. Did you say 'evil skinwalkers'?"

"Yup," he said.

Just the word *skinwalker* made my heart beat faster. In my mind, I saw a blob of skin walking around without a body. Maybe this blob of skin would grab on to me, I thought, and never let go. Or spit out some slimy liquid that would sting me like a jellyfish. My mind was suddenly filled with horrible ideas.

My dad always says that when you're scared, you should think of something funny to take your mind off being scared. I tried to make up a joke.

Knock, knock.

Who's there?

Skinwalker.

Skinwalker who?

I couldn't think of one funny answer to that question.

CHAPTER 6

I'll admit that I was scared, but Luna looked like she was going to faint. Her eyes grew wide, and her voice trembled when she spoke.

"These skinwalkers, are they as bad as they sound?" she asked Rio.

"The legend is that skinwalkers are people who can change their shape into any animal they desire," Rio said. "They often appear as coyotes or bears or crows."

"Will they hurt you?" I asked, telling

myself that I didn't believe any of this.

"They are evil witches," Rio said. "They roam these hills with harmful thoughts. They leave no tracks and can never be caught."

"But you've never actually seen one, right?" Luna said.

"We are told you must never look a skinwalker in the eye or you will be cursed forever," Rio answered.

Luna actually shuddered.

"Okay, let's not get crazy," I said. "As far as we know, there is no such thing as a skinwalker."

"Strange things happen out here in the desert," Rio said, gazing off into the distance. "I never thought I'd see an orange pig with a bucket on his head, but I'm looking at one now. For all I know, that pig could be a skinwalker."

On a nearby hill, trudging through the dirt toward us, was Chives.

"Wait here," I said to Luna and Rio.

I took off running and met Chives, guiding him behind a bush where we could not be seen.

"Hello, Master Tiger," he said. "I see you've found a guide. Well done."

"Where have you been, Chives?"

"I floated off while we were in the tunnel," he said. "And if I do say so myself, I had a most unfortunate landing. I believe I ripped my hiking shorts."

He turned around, and I could see his curly tail sticking out of the hole in his shorts.

"Listen, Chives," I said. "I need you to do me a favor. I'm going to ask that man, Rio, to help us find David. When we're with him, please don't talk."

"Not talk?" Chives protested. "But I have such a lot to say."

"Save it until we're alone," I said. "And one more thing. Could you try to walk on all fours?"

"Like a real pig?" Chives seemed very insulted. "I would be so embarrassed."

"Please, Chives. We don't want Rio to be suspicious. He already thinks you may be some kind of evil spirit."

Chives wasn't happy, but he agreed. I led him back to Luna and Rio. Even though he tried to trot like a pig, he tripped a few times over his hooves.

"Rio," I said. "This is our pet pig. We call him Chives."

"That bucket's mighty strange, but otherwise he looks like a fine pig," Rio said. "If you like orange pigs, that is." He gave Chives a playful poke in the belly.

"Oink," said Chives, shooting me an unhappy look.

"What brings you kids and your pig out

here?" Rio said.

"We've come to New Mexico to find our friend, David Dots," I answered.

"He's about thirteen years old."

"You mean the kid who collects arrowheads?" Rio said.

"That's him," Luna said.

"I saw him here yesterday. He knew all about Cerro Pedernal. Knew that it means 'flint hill.' Knew that local Native people have used the flint at the top to make arrowheads and tools. He was mighty excited about climbing it."

"Is there a trail going up there?" I asked.

"Hopefully one that the skinwalkers don't know about," Luna added.

"There's a trail," Rio said. "You pick it up about a half mile down this road."

"We're in a big hurry," I said. "Would you mind giving us a lift to the trail?"

"I guess I can help you out," Rio said. "You kids get in front. The pig rides in back."

I saw Chives frown.

"Oh, he won't mind a bit," I said, giving Chives a look. "Oink," he said, loud enough for everyone to hear.

We loaded Chives into the back of the pickup, and Luna and I slid into the front seat. The truck bumped along the dusty road, while Rio sang that song I'd heard in the tunnel. The closer we got to Pedernal, the taller it looked. Luna stared out the window. I don't know if she was looking for David or checking for signs of skinwalkers. Probably both.

We followed the road until it became so narrow we could go no farther. We pulled to a stop beside a meadow at the base of a steep slope.

"That's the trail to the summit," Rio said, pointing to a rocky path. "It's short but very steep. When you get to the top, it's all rock. There's a cave just before the capstone. If you find it, you can cross through to the summit. But don't dillydally. Thunderstorms blow in fast around here. You don't want to be up on the mountain during a lightning strike."

Wow, that was a lot to worry about. Steep trails, thunderstorms, lightning strikes. And Rio wasn't done yet.

"Remember," he said, "If you see any coyotes or bears, don't look them in the eyes."

I couldn't even glance at Luna. I could hear her whispering to herself. "I am brave, I am brave."

We climbed out of the truck and unloaded Chives from the back. I waved as Rio drove off in a cloud of dust.

Chives reached into the pocket of his shorts and pulled out his gold watch.

"It's nine minutes after four," he reported. "We don't have a minute to waste. We've got to climb to the summit, find David, and get back down by five o'clock."

"And don't forget that we have to run down the road to get back to our landing place," Luna added.

"What are we waiting for?" I said. "Let's move!"

We hurried over to the trailhead to begin our climb. We hadn't taken two steps when Luna suddenly stopped in her tracks and let out a scream.

"Tiger, look," she cried.

Lying on the ground in front of us was a cow skull. Its bones were bleached white from the sun, its long horns filled with holes from years of wind and dust storms.

Is this a warning? Should we turn back?

I wasn't sure. But deep in my heart, I knew that finding a cow skull in our path was definitely not a good sign.

CHAPTER 7

A dusty wind blew through the pine trees as the three of us stared at the cow skull, trying to decide whether to continue or turn back.

"I have an idea," Luna said. "Let's call David's name. If he hears us, he'll come down here."

We counted to three and all screamed together.

"David! David!"

There was no answer.

"I bet it's really windy on the mountain top," I said. "He probably can't hear anything with the wind howling all around him."

"We can't just stand here and let the hour tick by," Chives said. "I suggest we take a vote."

"All in favor of going up the mountain, raise your hand," I said.

"Or your hoof," Chives added.

We all voted to go ahead, even Luna.

"I see you voted yes even though you're scared," I said to her. "It takes a lot of courage to do something you're afraid of."

"My grandma says that real courage is being afraid but going on anyway," Luna answered. "Besides, I have Grandpa Arturo's drum to protect me."

She picked up a stick and pounded on the drum. Suddenly, the leaves in a nearby tree rustled, and a black crow flew out and shot across the sky.

"Don't look it in the eye," Luna warned.

We set out on the trail. At first, the path

was mostly dirt, but as we climbed higher,

more rocks began to appear. The valley below was so beautiful. Patches of brown and red earth were dotted with green trees that looked like bunches of broccoli from high up.

"Watch your step," I called as the path grew steeper. "Hold on to the rocks."

Suddenly, I heard a crash, followed by the sound of something hitting the ground.

"Look out!" Luna yelled. "It's a rockslide."

One of the rocks above had come loose. As it tumbled to the earth, it smashed into fragments. Other rocks followed. Some rolled down the steep slope, while some fell through the air.

"Duck!" I yelled.

Luna jumped aside, covering her head with her hands. The rocks flew past her, but one landed on top of Chives's head.

"Chives, are you okay?" Luna asked.

"I don't know," he said. "This bucket is stuck on my head."

Luna and I climbed down to help him. We grabbed the bucket and pulled, but it didn't budge. It was wedged tightly against his face. We pulled again.

"Ouch," he said. "You're hurting me."

A clap of thunder echoed around us. As if from nowhere, a huge gray thundercloud appeared. Lightning shot across the sky, followed by a pounding rain. It was so heavy that we could barely see the path beneath our feet.

"Chives," I said. "Can you stand on your head?"

"I could in my youth," I heard him

mumble into the bucket.

Luna gave me a *what are you talking about?* look.

"Basic science," I explained. "Water will make his head smooth, and smooth objects create less friction."

"Speak English, Tiger," Luna said.

"Sometimes when my mom tries to take her rings off, they get stuck on her finger," I said. "She runs her hands under water to make her fingers slippery, and then the rings slide right off."

"Oh, I get it," Luna said. "Why didn't you say that?"

Together, we helped Chives turn upside down. It wasn't hard for him to stand on his head because the bucket gave him a nice, flat surface to rest on. Some of the rainwater

seeped into the bucket in the little spaces
between his head and the sides.

"Move your head," I said to him. "Let the
water swish all around."

We sat him up. Grabbing the bucket,
we moved it from side to side, letting the

rainwater make the inside all slippery.

"You okay in there?" Luna asked Chives.

"My snout is certainly getting a good scrubbing," he said.

We wiggled the bucket some more, then *pop*, off it came.

"Oh, that's much better," Chives said, rubbing his face with his hooves. When he caught sight of the sharp rock lying on the ground next to him, he gasped.

"Is that what hit me?" he asked. "I could have been killed."

"But you weren't." Luna threw her arms around him in a huge hug I call the Luna Special. She put the bucket on his head.

"My accident has made us lose precious time," Chives said. "We have to move quickly."

"The path is slippery," I said. "Everyone has to be super careful."

Slowly, we inched our way up, one footstep at a time. The rain stopped just when we reached the end of the trail. The rest of the way to the top of Pedernal was nothing but a solid rock cliff.

"We can't climb that," I said. "It's straight up."

"Look," Luna said. She pointed to a ledge near us, about six feet long. At the other end of the ledge, you could just make out a hole in the black rock. "That must be the entrance to the cave Rio described. All we have to do is climb across this ledge, and we'll be at the mouth of the cave."

"That's a very narrow ledge for a very round pig," Chives said.

"You can do it," Luna told him. "Hold the mop out in front of you for balance."

I took the first few steps onto the ledge. Luna followed me. Chives, holding the mop out in front of him like a tightrope walker, went last. We pressed against the rock wall. It was a long way down. The trees in the valley no longer looked like broccoli. They looked like tiny green peas.

"Um . . . Luna," I whispered. "I have a secret to tell you."

"What is it, Tiger?"

"I'm afraid of heights," I whispered.

"What a time to tell me!" she whispered back. "Remember what my grandma said."

"About saying thank you?"

"About courage. Be afraid, but do it anyway."

I took a deep breath.

"I am brave," I whispered to myself.

Suddenly, we heard something howl. It definitely wasn't the wind. It sounded like an animal—a close-by animal! I saw a shadow of a four-legged creature behind a nearby tree. Luna saw it, too.

"I think it's a coyote," I whispered.

"What if it's a skinwalker?" Luna sounded so scared.

I could see the mop shaking in Chives's hand.

"Stay completely still," I said to him.

"And no matter what," Luna whispered. "Do not look that creature in the eyes."

Chives let out a frightened squeal.

"Luna," he said. "I already did."

CHAPTER 8

The coyote was crouched behind the tree, watching us. He was the size of a German shepherd, with a tan coat and yellow eyes. His tail was low to the ground, and he swung it back and forth.

Luna never lifted her eyes to look at the coyote.

"Skinwalker," she called out. "Go away."

The coyote growled and took a step forward. Chives's mop was shaking so much he could barely hold it. He edged closer to Luna. His mop accidentally hit the drum that was strapped to her back. It made a loud bang.

The noise stopped the coyote in his tracks. He looked at the drum with his squinty yellow eyes.

"Hit it again," Luna whispered to Chives.

Chives did, this time on purpose. The coyote howled.

"Play something, Chives," Luna said. "Beat the drum."

Chives held on to his mop and, using it like a drumstick, pounded the drum with all his might.

Womp, womp, womp.

"More," Luna said.

Womp, womp, womp. Ba-room. Ba-room. Donk-a-donk-donk.

As the drumbeat grew louder, the coyote began to back up. He raised his face to the sky and howled. Then he turned and ran. He bolted across the rocky side of the mountain and disappeared into a thicket of pine trees.

"He's gone," I whispered, taking a deep and much needed breath.

"Grandpa Arturo's drum protected me," Luna said. "His spirit is with me."

That's when we heard the voice, calling

to us from the mountaintop.

"Who's down there?" it said. "Who's that drumming?"

I recognized that voice. It was David Dots!

"David!" I shouted. "It's us. Tiger and Luna."

"Where are you?"

"Down here on the ledge. We're pretty scared."

"Don't move," David said. "I'm coming to help you."

We stood perfectly still. Within a few minutes, David appeared at the mouth of the cave.

"I'll reach out to you," he said, standing on the ledge and bracing himself against some boulders with his feet. "Hold my hand. You've only got five or six more steps."

I went first. Holding
David's hand helped steady
my steps. Luna went next.

When we were both safe at the mouth of the
cave, David threw his arms around us.

"I can't believe you're here," he said. "Did
my mother send you?"

"We can't talk now," I said.

"We have a friend who's still on the ledge."

We all looked over and saw the mop handle edging along the ledge, followed by Chives. He was taking tiny steps. Suddenly, Chives lost his balance and let go of the mop. We heard it clatter down the rocky face of Pedernal.

"We've got you, Chives," Luna said. She grabbed one hoof and I grabbed the other, and with David's help, we pulled him to safety.

"Thank you, children," said Chives. "You saved my life once again."

David took a moment to look Chives up and down.

"Who are you?" he said. "Or should I say, what are you?"

Chives looked at David, and his eyes filled with tears.

"Oh, Master David," he said. "It's really you. I never thought I would see the day when I would finally get to meet you. Your mother is right. You have the face of an angel."

Chives threw his stubby arms around David and hugged him hard. Never one to say no to a good hug, Luna threw her arms around both of them. I'm not the world's best hugger, but I have to confess, I joined in, too.

"Let me introduce myself," Chives said.

"I am Chives, your mother's butler. I was spit out of a painting at the same time you were sucked into one, exactly fifty years ago to the day."

"So that's why you're orange," David said. "Because you were a work of art?"

"Exactly," Chives said.

"Chives wanted to come with us, to help find you," I said.

"But how did you know where I was?" David asked.

"Your mom copied the Georgia O'Keeffe painting of Cerro Pedernal and put it in the fantastic frame," Luna said. "When we heard you collected arrowheads, we figured you'd be up here at the top where the flint is."

"You're not going to believe the treasures

I've found," David said. "Come look."

We ducked into the cave. David kneeled down and put several arrowheads on the ground in front of us. He pointed to one proudly.

"This one is made from flint and is really old," he said. "Maybe even from Paleo times." He held up another even sharper piece of stone. "I think this one is actually a spear tip. I can't wait to get home and read all about it."

"Home?" Luna said. "Does that mean you're coming home with us?"

David hesitated.

"Well, maybe not today," he said. "I'm having a great time up here. But some day I will."

"David, my boy," Chives said. "Do you know what today is? It's your mother's eightieth birthday."

"Oh, now I remember," David said. "I got pulled into the painting on her birthday. I never even got to give her the card I made."

"For all these years, I have taken care of your mother," Chives said, putting a hoof on David's shoulder. "Made her daily tea. Mixed her paints. Tended to her when she was ill. Listened to her stories about you. Loaned her my handkerchief when she needed to cry."

David put down his arrowhead and listened carefully.

"She is a difficult woman to be sure," Chives went on, "but I have grown to love her. By loving her, I have come to love you. Her one wish is to have you come home. Therefore, my one wish is to see the two of you together again."

"I've been meaning to come home," David said. "I almost did a couple of times. Ask Tiger and Luna, they'll tell you."

"Then today is the day, David," Chives said. "It's her birthday. There is no better birthday gift you could give her than yourself."

"She really misses me that much?" David asked softly.

"Her heart is broken without you," Chives answered.

We were all silent. David got up and

paced back and forth. I could see
that this was not an easy
decision for him.

"Time is growing short,
David," Chives said. "Now
is the moment for you to do
the right thing. Let me take
you back home. To the
place you're loved the
best."

"You're right, Chives,"
David said. "It's time. I'll come with you."

It's not often you see a pig smile. But
standing there in that cave on Cerro
Pedernal, Chives's smile was as big as the
whole New Mexico sky.

CHAPTER 9

"How long do we have to get back?" I asked Chives as we prepared to leave the cave.

He pulled out his pocket watch.

"Very little," he said. "It will take a mighty effort for us to make it down the mountain by five o'clock."

"I'm ready," David said. "Give me two seconds to grab the other arrowheads I collected."

He had only taken a few steps across the cave when we heard a frightening sound, a combination of a hiss and a rattle.

"What's that?" Luna whispered.

"It sounds like a rattlesnake," I said in a low voice.

I had never heard a rattlesnake for real, only on a TV special I had seen about snakes. But that noise was exactly the way they sounded on television.

"Nobody move until we see where it is," David whispered.

"I see it," Luna said. "It's behind a rock near your foot, David. And it's all coiled up."

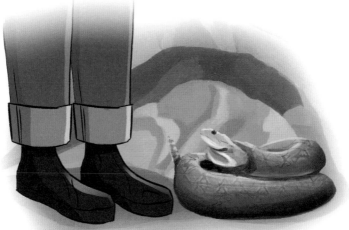

Oh no. Another thing I learned from that television show is that a rattlesnake's most dangerous strike comes when it's in the coiled position.

No one moved a muscle. We stood there, listening to that awful rattle grow louder. Suddenly, there was the sound of hoof steps followed by a tremendous clatter. I turned around just in time to see Chives bolt over to David, grab him, and pull him away from the snake. David and Chives fell to the ground and rolled across the cave, stopping only when they smashed into the opposite wall. Startled, the snake slithered away and disappeared through a crack in the cave wall.

Luna and I ran to David and Chives.

"Are you hurt?" I asked. "Did you get bitten?"

"I think I'm okay," David said.

David put his hand out, and Luna and I pulled him off the rocky cave floor. His shirt was torn and his elbow was cut, but other than that, he wasn't hurt.

"Chives," David said. "I could have died. You saved me. How can I ever thank you?"

David held his hand out to help Chives up. Chives didn't move.

"Hey, buddy," David said. "You're a hero."

Chives didn't answer. Quickly, we kneeled around him. I put my hands under his head. His eyes were closed. I couldn't tell if he was breathing.

"Chives," I pleaded. "Talk to me. Say something."

Ever so slowly, his eyes fluttered open.

"Is David all right?" he said very softly.

"He's fine," Luna said. "You pulled him away from the snake just in time."

"Thank goodness." A little smile crossed his face.

"Come on, buddy," David said. "Let me help you up. We've got some time-traveling to do."

David helped Chives into a sitting position, but when Chives tried to stand up, he couldn't. He squealed in pain and fell back onto the floor of the cave.

"It's my leg," he said.

Luna reached out and gently touched one of Chives's stubby legs.

"Does it hurt when I touch it?" she asked.

"Ow," was all he could say.

"Should we see if you can walk on it?" I asked.

"Let me catch my breath for moment," Chives said.

We waited, watching him breathe in and out. After a few breaths, Luna took him gently by the arm.

"Come on, Chives," she said. "You've got to try to walk."

"I did try, but I don't think I can, dear girl."

"My grandma says that if at first you don't succeed, try, try again."

"She's a wise woman. I'll give it a mighty effort."

Once again, Chives attempted to stand up, but he couldn't. The minute he put any weight on his leg, he doubled over in pain.

"I can't walk," Chives said. "You three are going to have to go on without me."

"I can carry you on my back," David said. "I'm strong."

David was strong, but not strong enough. When he tried to lift Chives and put him on his back, he couldn't even straighten up.

"Tiger," Chives said. "Get my watch and tell me the time, if you please."

I took the gold watch from his pocket and popped it open. It was getting very late, but I didn't want to tell him the time. If Chives knew how little time we had, he would make us go, make us leave him behind.

"We have enough time," I lied. "Let's try to get you up again. We're a team."

"We all know you'll never make it by five o'clock with me along," Chives said. "You must go, and go now!"

"But we can't leave you here alone," I said. "You're hurt. You need help."

David stood up and turned to face us.

"I'll take care of him," he said. "You two go home. I'll stay with Chives."

"No, young David," Chives said. "I can't have it this way. Your mother is waiting for you. You must go to her."

David kneeled next to Chives and patted his arm gently.

"You have stayed with my mother for all of the fifty years I've been gone," he said. "You have cared for her, served her, and loved her. Now it's time for our family to take care of you. For *me* to take care of *you*."

"But how?" Luna asked. "It's scary up here. You'll be alone. You've heard the stories. There may be ghosts or skinwalkers on this mountain. Not to mention the rattlesnakes."

"We'll be okay," David said. "Chives can rest here. I'll try to get help. And one day, as soon as you can, you and Tiger will return to bring us home."

"This isn't fair," Luna cried.

"But it's the right thing to do," David

said. "That's more important."

"You must go, children," Chives said. "Every second is precious."

It was hard to say good-bye to David, and almost impossible to say good-bye to Chives.

"Take care of yourself," Luna said to him. "We'll be back for you."

"We'll just be on the other side of the fantastic frame," I told him. I was so choked up, I could barely finish the sentence.

"We'll see you again," David said. "But only if you hurry now."

"We'll run like the wind," Luna said.

And without a backward glance, she took my hand and we left the cave, crossed the ledge, and ran down the trail as fast as our legs would go.

CHAPTER 10

I tried not to look at the watch as we made our way down the trail. I knew it would only make me more nervous to see the minutes ticking away. When we reached the bottom, Luna insisted that I give her the watch to check the time.

"It's five minutes to five," she said.

That was not good news. We still had to make it down the gravel road before the hour of power began. It didn't seem possible. I looked around, hoping for a miracle.

And one came.

An old car was coming down the road toward us. It seemed like it had appeared out of nowhere. Maybe the spirits of Cerro Pedernal were watching over us. The good spirits.

I happen to love cars, and this one was a classic.

"That's a Model A Ford," I said to Luna.

"I don't care if it's the Batmobile," Luna said. "As long as it's running."

We waved our hands and the car pulled up next to us. The driver was a woman about my grandmother's age. Her hair was pulled straight back, and she was wearing a black cowboy hat and a long black skirt.

"Excuse me, ma'am," Luna said. "Would you mind giving us a ride up the road?"

The woman leaned over and opened the door. "Hop in," she said. "I was just heading over to Ghost Ranch, which is in the same direction."

As we climbed in, we saw a cow skull on the passenger seat, just like the one we had seen at the entrance to the trail. Luna nearly jumped out of her skin.

"Oh, don't be frightened of that," the woman said with a laugh. "It won't hurt you. I just like to paint them."

We squeezed into the back, behind the passenger seat. I had only seen Model A Fords in pictures. This woman sure didn't take good care of hers. It was really messy in there, piled up with paints and brushes, not to mention cow skulls.

"Right up there would be fine," Luna

said, pointing to a flat stretch of road.

The woman pulled over and let us off.

"Thank you so much for the ride, Miss . . ."

"O'Keeffe," she said. "But everyone here calls me Georgia."

Just like that, she was gone, chugging down the road in her Model A Ford.

"Luna, that was Georgia O'Keeffe," I said. "Isn't that amazing?"

"Yes, but it's going to have to be amazing some other time," she said. "I checked the watch. We have one minute."

We could still see the marks on the gravel where we had landed, exactly an hour before. We lay down right on top of them and waited.

Gradually, the ground started to rumble.

The colors of the New Mexico sky began
to swirl—first blue, then gray, then all the
colors of the rainbow at once. I felt myself
floating above the road. I reached out and
grabbed Luna's hand.

"Are you ready?" I said.

"The hour of power is ending!" she
called. "Here we go!"

A strong gust of wind picked me up and spun me around. It was like a roller-coaster ride, but without the roller coaster. I opened my eyes for a second. Far below, I saw Cerro Pedernal rising up from the valley, its flat top hiding the secret cave where Chives and David would stay.

That was the last thought I remember having. The next thing I saw was two eyes staring into mine. They belonged to Viola Dots.

I sat up and looked across her living room at the painting of Cerro Pedernal. The hole was still there, but I could see it beginning to close.

"Luna!" I called.

With her arms out in front of her like Superman, Luna came bursting through the

hole in the painting and skidded to a stop
right in front of me. Viola Dots ran to us.

"Where are the others?" she asked.

"Chives got hurt," I said.

"Oh no!" Viola cried. "What happened?"

"He can't walk," I explained. "David was going to come home with us, but he stayed behind to take care of Chives."

Viola ran to the painting and touched its surface, but the hole had closed up. "They're both gone now," she said. "David! Why did you do this?"

"Because your son is the kindest person I've ever met," Luna said. "He's a good son and an even better friend."

Viola began to cry.

"They're safe," I told her. "They're in a cave on Cerro Pedernal."

"But I was counting on today," Viola cried. "It's my eightieth birthday. I'm growing old. I may never be able to see my son again. Or Chives. That foolish pig. How I love him, too."

She held her face in her hands and began to sob.

"All I ever wanted for my birthday was to have David back," Viola cried.

"And you will," I said. "Luna and I will go back for them. That's a promise."

Luna went to Viola to give her a big Luna Special hug.

"I'm so sorry," she said. "You shouldn't have to be this unhappy on your birthday."

"Maybe we can make it a little better," I said. "We have a surprise for you."

"We do?" Luna asked, giving me a confused look.

"Yes, we do. It's not as good as having your son back, but it might help a little. My mom baked a special birthday cake. She wants to bring it over to you."

"I haven't had a birthday cake in fifty years," Viola said. "But she can't come here. She'll see the frame."

"Then you come to our house for your birthday party," I said.

"I don't think I can go outside, Tiger. After all these years, I'm afraid."

"Just keep saying 'I am brave,'" Luna said. "That's what I do."

Luna took Viola by one arm, and I took the other. We guided her across the living room and out the front door. Of course, who was waiting on the sidewalk but stupid Cooper Starr. He stuck his tongue out at her, like the jerk that he is.

"Excuse me a minute," Luna said.

She flew down the path and marched up to Cooper Starr. Putting her hands on her hips, she got right in his face and let loose. I couldn't hear what she was saying, but I can tell you this: Cooper Starr jumped on his bike and rode away very fast.

Luna came back up the path and held her hand out for Viola.

"That's taken care of," she said.

"You're quite a girl," Viola smiled.

We walked Viola over to our duplex. Luna's grandmother was outside gardening, and my mom was waiting at the door.

"You must be Viola," my mom said.

"I hear it's your birthday."

"Feliz cumpleaños," Señora Lopez added.

"Please, come inside," my mom said.

Luna's grandmother stood up, linked her arm in Viola's, and walked her into our kitchen. Viola's birthday cake was waiting for her. Unfortunately, so was my sister, Maggie.

"You have a lot of candles to blow out," the little blabbermouth said to Viola. "That's because you're so old."

"Maggie!" my mom said. "That's not nice."

"Oh, that's all right," Viola said, to my surprise. "I like an honest child."

My mom brought the cake to the table and lit the candles.

"Make a wish," Maggie said.

"There's only one thing that I want for my birthday," Viola said. She looked at Luna and me. We knew that she was wishing for her son to be with her again.

She took a breath and blew all the candles out.

"Hooray, that means your wish will come true," Luna said.

As we ate our birthday cake, I thought of David and Chives. There we were, in our warm, safe, happy kitchen. And there they were, in a cold, damp cave with the wind roaring and the coyotes howling. I hoped the good spirits of Cerro Pedernal were watching over them.

It made me happy to see Viola enjoying her cake and being among friends. Suddenly, it struck me that my wish was the same as hers—to bring David and Chives home safely from that ghostly mountain so far away.

It was a big wish.

And it was up to Luna and me to see that it came true.

ABOUT THE PAINTING

Georgia O'Keeffe (American, 1887-1986). *Red Hills with the Pedernal*, 1936.
Pastel on paper mounted to wood-pulp board, 21-1/2 x 27-1/4 in. (54.6 x 69.2 cm).
Brooklyn Museum, Bequest of Georgia O'Keeffe, 87.136.4.

Red Hills with the Pedernal
by Georgia O'Keeffe

Georgia O'Keeffe is one of the most famous
artists of the twentieth century. She was
born in 1887 in Sun Prairie, Wisconsin, and
grew up on a farm where she learned to
love the land. Later in her career, she would
become fascinated with the landscape of

the badlands of New Mexico. She would walk the desert and hills, or drive in her Model A Ford, and paint what she saw. The painting in this book, *Red Hills with the Pedernal*, depicts a real mountain in the high desert of New Mexico. Georgia painted many versions of this beautiful flat-topped mesa. "It's my private mountain," she said. "It belongs to me. God told me if I painted it enough, I could have it."

When Georgia was starting out, it was very unusual for a woman to be a serious artist. Georgia was a pioneer. She studied art at the Art Institute of Chicago and the Art Students League in New York City. In 1916, some charcoal drawings she had done were discovered by Alfred Stieglitz, a well-known gallery owner in New York

City. He displayed her work in his gallery, where her talent was discovered by the art world. Georgia and Alfred fell in love and were married in 1924. By that time, Georgia had begun to create her famous large-scale paintings of natural forms.

Georgia O'Keeffe never painted people. She painted architecture, from the skyscrapers of New York City to the patio of her New Mexico home. She is best known for painting large close-ups of colorful flowers. She painted clouds and rocks and shells and bleached-out animal bones. She was fascinated with landscapes as well, and she came to specialize in the rugged land of northern New Mexico.

Georgia O'Keeffe's fascination with New Mexico began in 1929, when she traveled there in New York City to stay with a friend. Every summer after that, she returned to New Mexico to paint, until she moved there permanently in 1949 after her husband's death. She had two homes: a summer home in Ghost Ranch and a full-time home in the village of Abiquiú. For over twenty years, she painted the white cliffs, the red mountains, and the vast blue skies of New Mexico.

Georgia O'Keeffe produced over two thousand works of art in her lifetime. She was one of the first women to receive her own exhibition at New York City's world-famous Museum of Modern Art. When Georgia O'Keeffe died in 1986, her ashes were scattered from the top of her beloved Cerro Pedernal.

ABOUT THE AUTHOR

Lin Oliver is the *New York Times* best-selling author of more than thirty books for young readers. She is also a film and television producer, having created shows for Nickelodeon, PBS, Disney Channel, and Fox. The cofounder and executive director of the Society of Children's Book Writers and Illustrators, she loves to hang out with children's book creators. Lin lives in Los Angeles, in the shadow of the Hollywood sign, but when she travels, she visits the great paintings of the world and imagines what it would be like to be inside the painting—so you might say she carries her own fantastic frame with her!

ABOUT THE ILLUSTRATOR

Samantha Kallis is a Los Angeles–based illustrator and visual development artist. Since graduating from Art Center College of Design in Pasadena, California, in 2010, her work has been featured in television, film, publishing, and galleries throughout the world. Samantha can be found most days on the porch of her periwinkle-blue Victorian cottage, where she lives with her husband and their two cats. More of her work can be seen on her website: www.samkallis.com.